Sports Riddles

JOSEPH ROSENBLOOM

Sports Riddles

ILLUSTRATED BY
SAM Q. WEISSMAN

HARCOURT BRACE JOVANOVICH, PUBLISHERS
NEW YORK AND LONDON

Printed in the United States of America

LIBRARY OF CONGRESS CATALOGING IN PUBLICATION DATA
Rosenbloom, Joseph.
Sports riddles.
Summary: A collection of riddles relating to
baseball, basketball, boxing, bowling, football,
track and field, and other sports.
1. Riddles, Juvenile. 2. Sports—Anecdotes, facetiae,
satire, etc. [1. Riddles. 2. Sports—Anecodotes, facetiae,
satire, etc.] I. Weissman, Sam Q., ill. II. Title.
PN6371.5.R6135   796′.0207   81-7232
ISBN 0-15-277994-9   AACR2
FIRST EDITION   B C D E

Sports Riddles

Baseball

In which part of a ball park do you find the whitest clothes?

— *The bleachers*

What are the best baseball socks?

— *Socks with runs in them*

What is a baseball dog?

> — *A dog that wears a muzzle, catches flies, chases fowls, and beats it home when he sees the catcher*

What is the difference between a baseball player and a crazy pilot?

> — *One bats flies; the other flies bats.*

Two baseball teams played a game. One team won but no man touched base. How come?

> — *They were all-girl teams.*

Which is the slowest ball game?

— *Baseball. Players can score even with a walk.*

When do you have baseball eyes?

— *When you bat an eyelash*

Why couldn't anyone drink soda at the double-header baseball game?

— *The home team lost the opener.*

What batted baseball is a parent?

   — *A pop fly*

What makes music in the Baseball Hall of Fame?

   — *A record player*

What is the biggest jewel in the world?

   — *A baseball diamond*

How do you hold a bat?

> — *By its wings*

What is the biggest fly swatter?

> — *A baseball bat*

What has eighteen legs, red spots, and catches flies?

> — *A baseball team with measles*

Why did the silly kid take his baseball bat to bed?

 — *He wanted to hit the hay.*

What animals do you find at every baseball game?

— *Bats*

In which inning is the score always 0–0?

— *In the op-ening*

What insect is found on the grass in ball parks?

— *A ground fly*

Why was the baseball player arrested?

— *He stole bases.*

Does it take longer to run from first base to second, or from second base to third?

— *It takes longer to run from second base to third because there's no shortstop in the middle.*

Why do frogs go to baseball games?

— *To catch the flies*

Why was night baseball started?

— Bats like to sleep in the daytime.

What kind of inning do you have in a ghost baseball game?

—*A fright-ening*

Why was the baseball player taken along on the camping trip?

— *They needed someone to pitch the tent.*

Which baseball player wears the biggest shoes?

— *The one with the biggest feet*

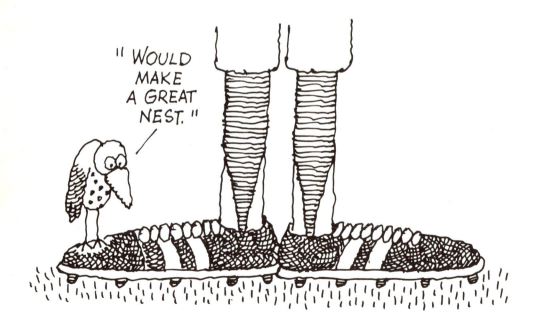

What kind of baseball game does a two-headed monster watch?

— *A double-header*

Where do catchers eat their meals?

— *On home plates*

What happened when the prince missed the ball?

— *He couldn't dance with Cinderella.*

What would you get if you crossed a lobster and a baseball player?

— *A pinch hitter*

Did you hear the joke about the pop fly?

　　— *Never mind. It's way over your head.*

What baseball hit belongs in a zoo?

　　— *A lion drive*

What do you find on a baseball team and on a table?

　　— *A pitcher*

Why is the ball park the coolest place in warm weather?

— There are fans in the stands.

What do absent-minded umpires do before they eat?

— *They brush off their plates.*

Who was Count Dracula's favorite person on the baseball team?

— *The bat boy*

What team cries when it loses?

— *A bawl (ball) club*

What famous ancient Greek played baseball?

    — Homer

What should you do if you don't succeed at first?

    — Try second

Why was Robin kicked off the baseball team?

    — He forgot his bat, man.

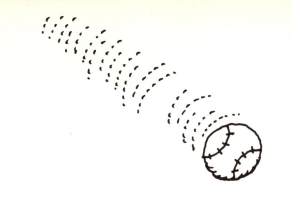

Why was Cinderella kicked off the baseball team?

— *She ran away from the ball.*

What do you do with a green baseball player?

— *Wait until he ripens*

Who lives under trees and hits home runs?

— *Babe Root*

What do you call a dog that catches baseballs?

— *A catcher's mutt*

What has two gloves and four legs?

— *Two baseball catchers*

What is the shortstop's favorite saying?

— *"If at first you don't succeed, try the outfield."*

What baseball player is welcome when you are out of breath?

— *A shortstop*

What kind of baseball throw is crazy?

— *A screwball*

What kind of baseball player is a father from Alabama?

— *A southpaw*

Why are baseball pitchers good at making flapjacks?

— *They know their batter.*

A man was afraid to go home because a masked man was out to get him. The masked man didn't carry a gun or any other weapon. What was the situation?

— *The man was on third base in a baseball game. The masked man was the catcher.*

If a basketball team were chasing a baseball team, what time would it be?

— *Five after nine*

Basketball

What happens if a seven-foot-tall basketball player sits in front of you at the movies?

— *You miss most of the movie.*

Why is basketball the sloppiest sport?

— *All the players dribble.*

Why are tall basketball players the laziest?

— *They are the longest in bed.*

What's a basketball player's favorite food?

— *Chicken in the basket*

Why did the police watch everyone on the basketball court?

— *They heard there were lots of sneakers there.*

What was the chicken farmer doing on the basketball court?

— *Looking for fouls (fowls)*

Why do people respect a seven-foot-tall basketball player?

— *They have to look up to him.*

Why did the silly basketball player bring a gun to the game?

— *He wanted to shoot the ball.*

Why are mummies good at basketball?

— *They are such big stiffs.*

Why is a seven-foot basketball player so tall?

— *Because his head is so far from his feet*

Which American poet is admired by basketball players?

— *Longfellow*

Boxing

What kind of book does a boxer like to read?

— *A scrapbook*

What is a boxer's favorite bird?

— *Duck!*

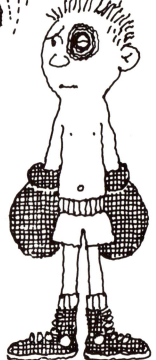

What kind of glove
can give you a black eye?

— *A boxing glove*

What ring is square?

— *A boxing ring*

Why are boxing matches popular?

— *They are hit shows.*

What is a fighter's favorite dog?

— *A boxer*

What would you get if you crossed a prize fighter and a meal?

— *A lunch box*

What is the difference between a boxer and a man with a cold?

— *A boxer knows his blows. A man with a cold blows his nose.*

What is a boxer's favorite drink?

— *Punch*

When is a boxer like an astronomer?

— *When he sees stars*

Why didn't the coward want to go into the kitchen?

   — *He was afraid of the lunch box.*

What happened when the ice cube fell on the boxer's head?

   — *It knocked him cold.*

What kind of match can knock you out?

   — *A boxing match*

Bowling

Why is bowling like a back street?

    — *It's played in alleys.*

Why is bowling such a quiet game?

    — *You can hear a pin drop.*

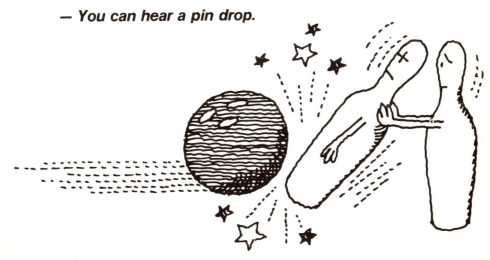

What kind of dog can be found around bowling alleys?

   — *A setter*

Why is bowling a slow game?

   — *The players have time to spare.*

What is a bowler's favorite food?

   — *Spare ribs*

What happens to old bowling balls?

— *They become marbles for King Kong.*

Football

Why is a football player's hand never larger than eleven inches?

    — If it were twelve inches it would be a foot.

What did the football say to the football player?

    — "I get a kick out of you."

What ghost helps win football games?

— *The team spirit*

What has twenty-two legs and goes "crunch-crunch"?

— *A football team eating potato chips*

What do you get if a football game is played on a potato field?

— *Mashed potatoes*

What one present does everyone kick about?

— *A football*

Which team has the largest football players?

— *The Giants*

Why was the football coach hated?

— *He was rotten to the end.*

Who are the happiest people at a football game?

— *The cheerleaders*

Why is it dangerous to play football on the lawn?

— *The grass is full of blades.*

How can you tell there's a 300-pound football player in your sandwich?

— *The sandwich is too heavy to lift.*

Why can't you play football if your watch is broken?

— *You don't have the time.*

Why did they call the bad football player "Judge"?

— *He was always on the bench.*

What has four wheels and carries a team?

— *A football coach*

How can you tell there's a football team in your bathtub?

— *It's hard to close the shower curtain.*

Where does a 300-pound football player sleep?

    — Anywhere he wants to

What do you say to a 300-pound football player with a short temper?

    — "Sir!"

Why did Cinderella's football team always lose?

    — Her coach was a pumpkin.

What is the difference between a football player and a duck?

— *You find one in a huddle, the other in a puddle.*

Why did the silly kid bring a string to the football game?

— *He wanted to tie the score.*

Where do they serve snacks to football players?

— *In the Soup-er Bowl*

Why are lollypops like a bad football team?

— *Anyone can lick them.*

What's the difference between a football player and a loaf of bread?

— *If you don't know, I won't send you out for bread.*

What three R's do cheerleaders have to learn?

— *Rah! Rah! Rah!*

Why is an airline pilot like a football player?

— Both want to make safe touchdowns.

What two things can't a football player have for breakfast?

— *Lunch and dinner*

When is cream like a defeated football team?

— *When it is whipped*

What color is a cheerleader?

— *Yeller (yellow)*

Track and Field

What colors do runners like?

— *Fast colors*

What does a polite jogger say when he leaves?

— *"So long. I've got to run now."*

When does the fastest runner lose the race?

— *When he wears socks guaranteed not to run*

Where do train engineers get together?

— *At a track meet*

Why did the giant jog every morning?

— *To get his extra-size (exercise)*

If Count Dracula raced, how would he finish?

— *Neck 'n neck*

Why should everyone run?

— *We all belong to the human race.*

Where do they keep long sticks?

— *In a pole vault*

How did the lazy man win the race?

— *He let his nose run.*

Who trains locomotives to run?

— *The track coach*

What kind of sand would you put in your shoe if you wanted to run faster?

— *Quicksand*

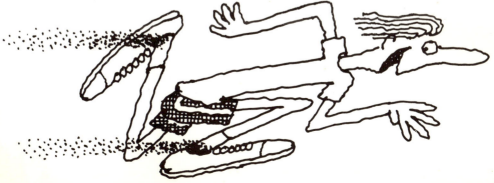

Sports Roundup

When does a horse do gymnastics?

— When it turns cart wheels

Why is it hard to drive a golf ball?

— It doesn't have a steering wheel.

Where do judges go to relax?

— *The tennis court*

What kind of pool can't you swim in?

— *A car pool*

What is the tallest building for sports officials?

— *The Umpire State Building*

What is a fencing master's favorite meal?

— *Lunge*

What injury do Olympic athletes often get?

— *A slipped discus*

What kind of trunks would you find in water?

— *Swimming trunks*

Why was the hockey player insulted?

— *The ice made cracks.*

What game is like a vegetable?

— *Squash*

What has eight wheels and carries one passenger?

— *A pair of roller skates*

Why did the karate expert hit the meat?

— *He wanted a lamb chop.*

Which player on the soccer team is not promoted in school?

— *The left back*

Where do golfers dance?

— *At a golf ball*

What's Count Dracula's favorite game?

— *Bat-minton*

What time is it when you are on a trampoline?

— *Spring time*

What famous Shakespearean character invented hockey?

— *Puck*

Why are waiters good tennis players?

— *They know how to serve.*

What game do girls dislike?

— *Soccer (sock her)*

What has two wings but doesn't fly?

— *An ice hockey team*

What kind of pajamas does a 400-pound wrestler wear?

— *Super-extra large*

How do you kiss a hockey player?

    — You pucker up.

Why are fish poor tennis players?

    — They don't like to get too close to the net.

Why did the golfer always carry three socks with him?

    — In case he got a hole in one

Which winter sport do you learn in the fall?

— *Ice skating*

When is a wrestler like a baby?

— *When he is pinned*

What kind of school would have a sign saying: PLEASE DO NOT KNOCK?

— *A karate school*

Why is tennis the loudest sport?

— *Everyone raises a racket.*

Why is a riddle about a football player the last one in this book?

— *Because he is . . .*

THERE IS STILL
POWER IN THE BLOOD

William W. Woods

To order additional copies of this book, contact:
Xlibris Corporation
1-888-795-4274
www.Xlibris.com
Orders@Xlibris.com
56725